Ti
&
Jane

ALEXIA ROWE

ISBN-10: 1530775396
ISBN-13:978-1530775392

CONTENTS

1 WHEN THE LIGHTS GO OUT

Jane lays awake under the freezing covers, her eyes hardly moving to blink. Barely any light shines in from the hallway, and she watches the door intensely with tired eyes. She pulls the edge of her thick comforter all the way up to her ears, and she sinks further into her white, down pillows. A look of horror right from the movies is plain across her face. However, her room is quiet, and the only sound is howling wind from outside. She is basked in darkness and can hardly see her surroundings, intensifying her fear and paranoia.

Her room is extremely neat, with only a few disregarded items lain randomly about the room, waiting to be put away. Strong scents of jasmine and lavender float around her room, and her dark wooden floorboards are still glossy from a recent wash and polish. A line of philosophical books are tucked neatly on the middle shelf of her bookshelf, while a line of fantasy and mystery hoard the shelf above. On the two last shelves below, are random items; An old dictionary and thesaurus lay abandoned on their sides, holes and rips in the covers portray Jane J Pipper as the sole owner of the books. An old forgotten teddy bear, a gift from her deceased mother, lay toppled over on the very bottom shelf, right next to a pile of journals. The floorboards creak every second moment, and the window groans against the forceful wind. Looking over at her closet, she can see something move against it.

Gasping, she sits up in bed and looks urgently at the closet. She feels her heart pumping wildly, and her fingers start to shake. A rising pressure appears in her throat and she feels a tightness closing around her neck. Unable to breath, she claws at her neck, only to find skin peeling under her fingernails, and the air suddenly pushing back into her lungs.

Shakily, she attempts to lay back down, and closes her eyes slowly. When she opens them again, her heart has slowed and her breathing calmed. When she looks closer at the waving object in the closet, she realizes it is just a sleeve that belongs to a blue sweater hanging inside the closet. Slowly, Jane settles back into bed and slowly inhaled and exhales.

Her eyes burst open moments later only to find her body continuously shivering uncontrollably. The temperature of the house has dramatically dropped, and there is still seven hours until sunrise. The thought of getting out of bed, and walking across the stone cold floor sends shudders down her back. Jane feels an imploding desire to scream. With a groan, she heaves herself out of bed and begins to make her way towards the closet.

Her feet turn to ice almost the second her feet touch the floor. Goosebumps raise on every inch of her skin, and her entire body has now gone into teeth rattling shivering. She hastily rubs her hands up and down her arms, however to no avail the rubbing creates no heat. She gives up quickly, and looks towards her closet.

She opens the door to her closet, and moves aside the thin, blue sweater. Instead, she grabs a much thicker sweater that is black, and pulls it over herself. She contemplates grabbing something more, but figures she shouldn't be too long. Then, she grabs her slippers from the corner, and pulls them onto her naked feet. The comforting feel of lukewarm fluff gave Jane hope, and she stiffly begins moving towards the bedroom door. While still cold, she opens the thick mahogany door and makes her way to the grand staircase. As she passes her brother's door, she hesitates, stops then knocks. A few seconds pass before she hears a rough holler from the other side.

"What?" Tim calls out from the other side of the closed door. She imagines him laying on his bed, half awake, yelling angrily at her with a sleepy look on his face.

Yelling back, she asks him, "can you open the door, please?" Then, she waits patiently and quietly. She hears sounds come from the other side and presses her ear against the door. From inside, shuffling, banging, and a muffled scream can be heard. Jane backs away from the door in surprise and horror. The doorknob rattles briefly before the entire door swings open and Tim steps out. He closes the door quickly behind him, and she is unable to see past his large, black bush of a head. Jane's eyebrows crinkle together and she twists her lips to the side. "Hello, brother," she says finally.

Tim narrows his oval eyes at her, and yawns loudly. Looking at him, she can't stop comparing. He and Jane are identical twins, with the same jet black hair and ice blue eyes. However, where her hair is long and thick, reaching well past her back and hitting her knees, her brother's hair is cropped short and barely reaches his ears. She keeps her hair soft and clean, whereas Tim's hair seems to always be greasy. They do in fact share the same body types; they both have slim figures with slight shoulders. The only difference between the two, besides the detail in hair, is their skin. While Jane's skin is ivory and glowing, Tim's skin is pale and grey. He appears quite malnourished, and looks like a walking skeleton half the time.

Jane stands there, staring at her identical brother. A warm feeling floods her brain, and she suddenly feels like she is falling. Attempting to gain footing, she reaches out and leans on the door frame for balance. Tim stares at her with mild distaste and curiosity. His upper lip curls and a line of yellowing, sharp teeth are revealed. "What do you want?" He growls through clenched teeth, and his arms are crossed tightly over his slim chest.

Jane suppresses a chill and steps away from Tim in surprise. Aggression is familiar when coming from Tim, however for some reason it still surprises her. Her arm hair rises and she picks at her skin with a finger nervously. She coughs into one hand, and looks at her brother with hope. Shivering, Jane steps closer to Tim, but he backs away from her. With a frown, she whispers, "the power is out."

Tim blinks at Jane slowly. "So?" He asks loudly, his eyes glowing with anger. "What are you waking me up for?"

" Well that means the heating is off. Dad won't be home until next week. We'll freeze before the sun rises tomorrow morning. I need your help to get the power back on." Jane looks at her brother with wide, blue eyes. Her entire body is taken over by a series of chills and shakes. She waits as her teeth clatter furiously, causing her jaw to ache. "Can you help me fix it, please?" She finally asks after five minutes of silence.

Curling his lip once more, Tim hisses in her face. The amount of anger and hostility filled in that single expression causes Jane to step back a step and almost trip over her own two feet. "You're so helpless," he hisses through clenched teeth. His hands are at his side, slightly outstretched in angry, threatening fists. A look of disgust is plain across his face, and Jane takes another step back as her entire body continues shaking. "Why can't you ever do anything on your own? You're such a helpless, stupid," Tim begins saying, each word coming out as a fresh slap across her heart. "Worthless little girl," Tim finishes sadistically, "no one will ever love you. There is nothing to love in you."

2 DON'T GO DOWNSTAIRS

The hallway is left in silence as both Tim and Jane stare at each other, both looks filled with extreme emotion. Jane, on the verge of crying, looks into Tim's identical blue eyes. She can sense rolling waves of anger and hatred towards her. For reasoning, she cannot find. Her lips shake as she attempts to question his actions, however no words spill out of her weak lips. She looks down the hallway, towards her bedroom, and contemplates going back to climb back underneath the covers.

The dawning knowledge that if she does do that, warmth will never come. Frustration fills her chest and a tear flows over and falls down her dry cheek. She looks up and down the hallway nervously, unaware of what to do or what to think. She knows the power is out, and she knows she needs it to be turned back on. She also knows she cannot do it on her own. However, she also knows her brother doesn't seem to want to help.

Jane hesitates before snapping back at him, "I could do it on my own!" Lying, she refrains from meeting his eyes. When she looks up, she see's Tim's eyes flash red with anger, literally. Jane gasps as she thinks her mind is beginning to play tricks on her. One moment, his eyes are ice blue, then the next they flash a brilliant, bright red that shocks Jane to her core. Then suddenly, they're back to being blue. Jane clears her throat, then in a shakier voice, she adds, "it's midnight. The moon is out, the sun is gone. I won't be able to see without our flashlight. Remember, Dad always says to bring someone at night to the shed. Otherwise, we'll get lost. Remember?"

"Oh, I remember," he replies coolly, and his eyelids drop slightly. He looks at her in a strange way, then gives her a twisted grin. "Shadows come out to play during the night."

Jane looks at Tim slowly before asking, "what?"

"You don't always have to listen to what Dad says, do you?" Tim says in a taunting voice, disregarding Jane's confusion. She looks at him with suspicious eyes, and takes a hesitant step towards the wall behind her. A chill winds around her legs and runs up her spine, and she shivers. Jane looks at Tim as he takes a step towards her, a malicious smile set across his lips, and moans softly. "What's wrong with going against the rules? Too scared to do anything wrong?" Jane takes a final step back and feels the ice cold wall hit her back. The low temperature seeps through her sweater and hits her skin like a bag of ice. Slowly, Tim bends and whispers in her ear, "doesn't it ever tempt you to be bad?" His words a caressing knife along her neck.

Jane shivers and gapes at her brother. "No, why would I do that?" He opens his mouth to speak, but a loud bang comes from down stairs. Shortly after, another bang follows. It sounds like the front door opening and closing loudly. Metal clanging echoes up the staircase and reaches their waiting ears. It persists, like an angry child throwing a tantrum and continuously banging the door. "What was that?" She asks while staring towards the staircase.

Jane's feet slowly shuffle forward, and her shoulder rubs against Tim's arm. She looks over at him quickly, and finds his eyes trained on the staircase. She forgets about Tim, and slowly creeps closer to the top of the staircase, and peers over to get the best view of the front door. As she leans over, she is able to see only a small corner of the front door, and watches with horror as it opens and closes loudly. The door slams back into the door frame, and it ricochets all around them. She doesn't see a hand causing the action. With a shaky intake of breath, she takes an immediate step away from the top of the staircase. She moves quickly to return back to the hallway, and looks to Tim for assistance.

His eyes remain locked on the staircase, and as she returns alongside of him, his eyes don't even twitch towards her. She listens with horror as the banging persists, and the entire house is filled with the chaotic noise. Dread and fear fills Jane tremendously, and she reaches out to hold onto Tim blindly. Her hand falls to her side, unable to reach his arm. As she looks over at Tim, her stomach flips to find a mischievous grin plastered across his face, and his eyes trained directly on her. "Tim?"

He doesn't say anything, and Jane freezes. Her eyes dart back and forth from her brother to the staircase. The banging still continues on, and she gains an urge to cover her ears. However, her body does not respond, and she stays motionless as Tim slowly creeps closer towards her and corners her against the wall. Both of his hands land on the wall, each one on either side of her head.

"What are you doing?" Jane asks, and her voice rises into a high pitched squeak. Heat rises to her face and her stomach twists and turns. She feels a rising pressure in her chest, and nausea overwhelms her.

"Calm down," he says, and Jane breathes loudly as she blinks at him. Tim stares down at her with ferocious eyes. Then, without warning, he grabs her and pushes her aside roughly. He begins making his way to the stairs, and after a moment of hesitation, Jane quickly scurries after him. She hangs onto his elbow as they descend the stairs, only for him to quickly shake her off. "Don't be such a baby," he says. Persistent, Jane grabs back onto him though, and while he tries to shake her off again, she holds on tight.

After realizing she wasn't falling off, he sighs and

continues making his way down the staircase, ignoring her as much as possible. With each step they take, the wood groans under their weight. Finally, the banging stops just before they can get a proper view of the door.

Jane sighs with relief when they finally arrive at the bottom of the staircase and she releases her hold on Tim. The two teenagers face the large, white door. Tim, with a look of fiery excitement that causes Jane to rethink her idea, stands with his feet spread far apart and looks quite determined. Jane stands slightly behind Tim, looking between the motionless door and her twin brother. Her ice blue eyes are wide with fear, and her lips have frozen shut.

They live in a large, victorian manor with their step father on a large, very old acreage. The Willington family; the grandparents to Jane's grandparents, bought the land out years ago. It has been said the family have been living on these grounds ever since. However, an unfortunate event grasped Jane's heart a mere four years ago, when her biological father died tragically of a heart attack. Her mother waited almost four years until getting married again. Jane remembers when she brought home her step-father, Ernesto.

Ernesto is a tall, broad shouldered man with shoulder length blonde hair, a constant five o'clock shadow covering his jaw, and piercing green eyes. When her mother remarried, Jane was upset at first, however learned to accept the sudden change in her life. Her mother and Ernesto knew each other for only a short month before getting married, and him moving into the manor. Shortly after, Jane's mother died from a tragic accident on a stormy night. Her and Ernesto had gone out for dinner, leaving at different times. He came back with a worried look on his face, asking where his wife is. The cops never did find her, Jane remembers terribly.

Jane remembers vividly her step father hiding in their bedroom for weeks. She would hear him howling in pain every night, and her heart would ache every time for him. Although she was in fact their mother, she felt a pain for Ernesto she wasn't aware she could feel. She knew how terrible he must miss their mother, for he loved her.

Due to the tragic events, Jane found herself left in the custody of Ernesto. Now, her and Tim live in the manor with him. She finds the house terribly quiet and lacking since the death of her mother, and constantly finds herself wishing for her return simply for the sound of her laugh. As Jane stands in the foyer, fear drenched in her gut, she once again wishes for her mother and father's return. As she looks at Tim, feeling an urge to reach out for safety, she knows she will not find what she is looking for from him.

Jane watches her brother creep slowly towards the front door. With far too much excitement and energy, he turns the brass knob and shakes the door, proving it is still locked and secure. Tim then shrugs, turns around, and looks at Jane. He rolls his eyes, as if she had made up the entire thing, then begins walking towards the marble corridor. As he makes his way towards the living area of the main level, Jane slowly returns to the bottom of the stair case.

Jane watches from the lowest step on the staircase as he disappears past a marble statue, and never returning on the other side. Jane waits for his face to reappear, but it never does. With horror, Jane gasps and takes a step towards the corridor. Something in her gut stops her from moving any closer, and she inhales slowly to attempt to calm herself.

"Tim!" She calls back, and waits for him to respond or reappear. He does neither. "What are you doing?! It isn't funny, alright? Come back here so we can fix the heat! Please?" Jane takes a step up onto the staircase instinctively when she doesn't hear a reply. She leans against the bannister as it digs into her side painfully, and she attempts to look down the corridor. She sees only a dark hall, with the four doors still closed. From this angle, she can see behind the statue now. Tim isn't there.

"Tim?" She calls out again, her words echoing around her. "I'm serious, Tim. This isn't even funny." With shaky hands and quivering lips, she adds weakly, "I'm going back upstairs now." Then, she lifts a hesitant foot and brings it up one step, her other foot quickly follows steadily. There is still no response, and Jane groans.

The temperature appears to still be dropping, and Jane's hands are going white. With a frustrated gargle, she takes a deep breath and slowly descends the few short steps. Looking down to ensure she doesn't trip, she tries to only focus on the task at hand; get to the floor. When she reaches flat land, she looks up with dread. Then, with one last hesitation, she goes to turn down the corridor in search of her twin brother.

She makes her way down the dark corridor, aware she is unable to see much in the windowless hall. There is no longer any moonlight seeping in, and she is careful not to trip over her own feet. With a hand on the wall, she slowly creeps through the hall, looking for the first door.

"What are you doing?" Jane comes face first with Tim immediately, without any warning. A small scream escapes her lips before he quickly slaps his hand on her mouth harshly. "Shut up!" He hisses, and she nods. He drops his hand, and her mouth is left stinging. She realizes Tim is looking at her with boredom and hatred.

"L-looking for you," she stutters from fright. "W-where did you go?"

"Nowhere," he replies tightly. "I've been standing here this entire time." A chill passes through Jane as she watches him closely. His eyes stay trained on her for a few short moments, then he rolls his eyes and shoves past her. He walks down the hallway and enters the foyer towards the coat closet. Jane quickly follows, glad to leave the dark hallway. She watches him open the closet door, and he reaches up to pull a thick dark jacket down. He pulls it on, then quickly zips it up. Jane moves to grab her winter jacket, but he holds a hand up to stop her. She waits. He then takes out a pair of winter boots and then promptly shuts the closet door shut.

"Where are you going now?" Jane asks him while stepping closer. "Outside?"

"Duh." He replies roughly, giving her a devilish glare that causes her to take a step back.

"I'll need my jacket and boots as well, then." She says quietly, unsure of another way to put it. Tim is blocking the closet door from her, and if she were to ask politely then he would never let her get her jacket. Frustrated, she waits for his response.

"No," he says finally, to her surprise. "You won't."

3 BLIZZARD

"What do you mean?" Jane asks, extremely creeped out and confused. Tim looks at her seriously, while she stares back, puzzled. The house is already freezing, she can't imagine how cold it will be outside. Her hands are shaking, and she tucks them under her armpits in a feeble attempt to hide her immobile limbs. "I need my jacket," she tries to say sternly, and attempts a determined expression. However, her lips are shaking and her words are barely tangible.

Tim's eyes flash red again, to Jane's surprise. Her mind continues playing tricks on her, why, she has no idea. His eyes return to their ice blue stance, and she shakes her head to focus. *Maybe I'm going crazy,* she thinks to herself.

"No, you don't." Tim then flashes a light in her face abruptly, and she attempts to block the light with her hand. "Come on, already. And shut up." He adds as an afterthought then grabs her by the arm roughly. Dragging her across the foyer towards the front door and not letting her grab any gear for herself, Tim forces her outside without any warning, in two seconds flat.

Too soon, she finds they are outside and a flurrying blizzard is falling down hard around her. She shivers uncontrollably, and as they step out onto the front porch her entire body starts to shake violently. In a weak attempt to keep warm, she wraps her short arms around her torso while silently regretting grabbing only one sweater from her closet. She glares at Tim, with his back facing her, but feels thankful for the progress.

"There," she says and points towards the bend that leads to the back yard. With the help of the flashlight she is able to see what direction the old pathway lies, and she takes a step towards the wobbly stones. Jane lands in thick, cold snow that reaches well past her ankles. Her small, thin slippers offer little protection from the elements. Unfortunately the snow piles higher than the top of her slippers, and it chills her ankles to the bone. More snow falls heavily, in thick, white puffs all around them, masking the view before them in white nothingness. Tim shining the light seems to only illuminate the snowflakes falling.

Jane looks down as she begins to feel a shocking wetness on her feet, and suppresses the urge to scream. Instead, she gasps quietly, as to not alert Tim, and continues walking down the path. Her slippers are beginning to soak, and she feels disease edging its way into her body and immune system. Fear is crawling all around Jane's chest, and all she wants to do is scream. *Why wouldn't he let her get a jacket?* Tim releases his hold on her as the gate to the backyard comes into view.

"Can I go get my jacket and boots quickly?" She asks while pointing in the direction of the front door with her thumb. She takes a tentative step away from Tim and the gate, only for his head to snap up seconds later with a ferocious growl playing on his paling lips.

"No," he says and turns his entire body back towards her. A small cry escapes her lips as he crosses the distance between them quickly and grasps her roughly by the elbow again, most likely leaving a dark, painful bruise. Tim hauls her towards the gate menacingly, away from the front door and her jacket. While she feels hope deflate in her chest, she ignores every screaming, aching urge to kick him where the sun don't shine.

This is your only way of getting the heat back on, she reminds herself sternly. Tim releases her and she falls against the fence. He reaches up and unlocks the frosted gate, and pushes it with his shoulder with a hard, growling push. The wooden gate creaks as it swings open, and Tim pushes her through the opening without any warning. She stumbles and almost falls into the snow, but gains her balance only to lose a slipper. She gasps as icy air hits her naked foot, and the tips of her toes begin to turn white. With a shriek, her naked foot lands in the cold snow.

Jane hears the gate slam shut, and two seconds later Tim is at her side. "Shut up!" He roars in her ear, scaring her half to death. She shrieks once more before falling backwards into the snow. In an attempt to break her fall, she turns to reach out her hands. Snow hits her face like a brick wall, and she struggles to get back up and breathe.

Jane, traumatized, looks up at her twin brother as he shines the only flashlight in her eyes. Unable to see, she looks down at herself and attempts to scramble back up. She ignores the screaming coming from her body, and waits for Tim to continue walking towards the shed. With a very slow intake of breath, she stands motionless while watching Tim to make the first move. To her surprise, he continues towards the shed. With a sigh of relief, she moves forward and briefly loses her balance and almost falls into the snow once more. Luckily able to find her footing first, she nervously follows Tim. "Come on, already. Stop being such a baby." Tim yells from over his shoulder, his words are harsh against the wind, and she winces.

"I'm not a baby," she whispers quietly to herself.

"Shut up," Tim responds and she quiets. Tears well up in her eyes but she refuses to let them spill over. They would only turn to ice, anyways."Stop being such baby," Tim says when he looks back at her.

Quietly so to not alert him, she mutters again, "I'm not a baby." She watches his shoulders tense up, but he does not look back at her or say anything further, to her relief. Quietly, he stomps through the snow. She follows suit, only to find her foot touching something soft yet hard at the same time. Looking down, she is relieved to find grass beneath her feet, instead of the concrete. Sighing, she is content they are no longer walking on the freezing pathway.

While the grass is still cold, it is not as harsh, and still allows a soft surface for her to walk on. Her toes feel like they are going to fall off, and her teeth keep chattering. They have already been outside for longer than ten minutes, and they are almost at the shed. *If her mother were here, the power would be back on by now,* she thinks. Jane finds herself thinking of what-if's, and she *knows* that if her mother were still alive, she wouldn't feel so alone. A sob shatters her chest and escapes her lips, Tim doesn't even bother looking back. The idea both upsets Jane, and relieves her at the same time.

She feels so alone.

Jane attempts to calm herself down for the rest of their long walk to the shed. For some reason the old structure was placed at the very back end of the field, right next to the forest. She can barely feel the bottom of her feet, and she is not sure what color her toes are anymore. With dread, she hopes they aren't black.

Finally, they arrive at the shed. It's aged wood is covered in black mold, and she can also see a dead mouse lying under a pile of snow by the side. She curls her top lip and moves towards the door. Tim pulls the door open and it groans loudly. As the thick wooden door opens achingly slowly, every second feels like an hour to Jane. Snow starts falling into the dark room as they enter, leaving a blanket of white at the opening. They leave the door open as Jane searches for the light switch without the aid of Tim's flashlight.

4 CREATURES MOVING IN THE NIGHT

The frozen wood is harsh on Jane's aching, burning feet, and she's unsure which is worse; the snow or the wood. Except for the flashlight in Tim's hand illuminating the space before him, the rest of the shed is blanketed in darkness. Jane rummages around blindly, hitting corners of desks and tables, as she searches for the light switch on the wall. While Jane looks for the light source, Tim walks around the room, not helping her. Somehow, she manages to find a cold hard panel with a switch, she presses it and the room is illuminated in a bright light. Jane finds herself thankful for the shed being on a separate power grid than the house.

Blinking from the sudden light, Jane looks around the shed. The shed used to belong to her biological father, he used it as a work shed to work on construction. When he passed, it was cleaned out and the only thing left in the structure was the generator. After her mother met Ernesto though, he took the opportunity to make this his own workshop, and now dirty, old tables reside in the same place where her father used to work.

Jane is surprised at her bitterness towards Ernesto, considering everything he has done for them both. He could have given them up to relatives, however, instead he took them under his wing and adopted them as his own. While she hasn't fully warmed up to him, she knows Tim has. It could be possible this is causing her resistance to trust Ernesto; his connection with Tim, but she doubts it.

Looking over at Tim, she finds he is not at the generator like she expected. Instead, he is at the aged work table. A fine layer of dust covers the crooked mahogany completely, despite only being in the shed for a short amount of time. He stands with his rigid back to her and his neck slightly bent. With her staring at his back, he is completely unaware of her gawking. The idea of him knowing frightens her, and she assumes she would start shaking if her body isn't already shaking violently from the cold. She watches as he slowly grazes the work table delicately, as if it were an antique instead of just an old work table. Rarely does she ever see Tim treat anything with this much delicacy, and the sight leaves her breathless. She watches with a curious glance as his long, pale fingers come up with a thick layer of black dust across the palm.

Bewildered, Jane gasps softly from the emotional

stricken Tim in the corner of the generator shed. It was such a strange, and quite uncomfortable situation for Jane, and she feels awkward standing in the opposite corner, unsure what to do. A peculiar, saddening look crosses over his face swiftly before disappearing into the rest of his emotions. While it peeks her curiosity, she doesn't say anything to him. Taking a step towards him, however, she offers a propped hand. She considers asking him what is bothering him, however she knows the only possible response he could distribute is him telling her to shut up.

Jane, shrugging, passes him with indifference and makes her way to the generator. Quickly forgetting about him, she works on focusing on the task at hand; Getting the power back on usually was easy and was resolved by a simple reconnection. She figures just because Tim escorted her here, doesn't mean he will help with the mechanical stuff. At the generator, she bends down and kneels softly on the hard, cold floor. From the front she studies the machine for the first time in her life as the prime mechanic.

The main, large tube is properly hooked up by the looks of it and she tugs on both ends to confirm, neither side comes loose. She leans back on her heals, unsure what else to do, since the machine remains not humming with power. Jane begins to fiddle with the sides, looking for any hidden wires or buttons, but finds none. Determined to find a solution, she continues searching on her hands and knees.

Pieces of her cold skin are beginning to blister, however with stubbornness she manages to ignore the agonizing pain. However, fifty minutes pass and she still can't hear the gentle hum of power. Jane huffs and sits back on her heels in disappointment. While she stares at the machine, brainstorming, something begins to shuffle behind her, without her awareness.

Creating too little of noise to reach her ears, the source of the movement continues to near her. It shuffles underneath a large pile of old, dirty newspapers. Every page contains an article regarding some type of wild animal. Beneath the newspapers, it begins to move towards Jane again quietly so as not to alert her.

"Tim?" Jane calls out when she finally gives up, and looks over at him. Tim starts, jerking out of a daydream. Suddenly looking alive, he slides off of the seat he was sitting on, leaving a trail of dirt behind on his jeans. A patch where he was sitting is left bare on the leather seat. Her eyes jump from the seat to her brother, and she watches his expression turn from distracted pain, to surprise, then suddenly to the familiar hatred and disgust he displays towards her.

"What?" He snaps at her and his dark hair falls down over his eyes. She can only see his crinkled nose and curled upper lip.

"Can you help me over here, please?" She asks politely, her voice light and patient. Tim groans, however surprisingly does come over to her to help with her and the generator. As he kneels, the thing begins to close more space between them, without her knowledge.

Tim looks at the generator with a look of boredom, his blue eyes are narrowed and look dead. Jane raises an eyebrow at him, and he looks at her strangely, as if asking her what to do. She watches as his eyes light up, as a brand new idea enters his head. His lips spread into a long, evilish grin that turns Jane's stomach into somersaults. The thought frightens her to her core. Suddenly, Tim then moves to the back and squeezes himself between the machine and the wall. From where she is on the floor of the other side of the generator, she can still see him from the front. However her view of him consists only of the top of his head and his long feet dangling from the side.

"Why are you over there?" Jane asks, unsure why he moved. All the connections are where she is, at the front of the generator. Where TIm is sitting, is a simple flat siding with possible warning and cautionary stickers.

"There's more connections over here," he replies simply, and her eyes narrow. However, she makes no move to get closer, and doesn't say anything to fight the lie. Shrugging, she slides away from the generator slightly, just to be safe. She leans against a dirty block of wood, completely unaware she is getting closer to the thing moving under the newspapers.

"Just let me know if anything changes," she says loudly enough for him to hear, but he doesn't reply. Jane sighs and scratches at her arms. Her entire face feels frozen, and every part of her body aches and moans with every small movement. With every new breath she inhales, it feels like it will be her last. The air feels so thin inside the shed, and she pulls at her shirt's neckline.

While she attempts to calm down, she listens to Tim fiddle around with what he called connections. A small bumps and groans can be heard from where he sits, and every now and then his feet twitch.

That's when she hears it out of nowhere. As Jane watches one of Tim's feet still slowly after a small twitch, she leans further against the wall of the shed. She sighs deeply, and with boredom watches the large puff of hot air leave her mouth into the cold atmosphere. Jane twists her lips to the side, and shifts forward. About to ask Tim for an update, she opens her mouth at the same time she hears a chilling creek right beside her.

5 PRINTS

Slowly, Jane turns her body towards the sound. When she turns her head to the left, she looks over to see the shed door moving in the wind, and her body instantly relaxes with relief. Feeling skittish, she turns away from the creaky old door and stares at Tim's feet again. His feet have not twitched yet, and she can no longer hear bumps and groaning. *Maybe he found the problem*, she thinks hopefully and smiles.

Jane scrambles up off of the dirty ground and wipes herself clean. Her hands sting where they slap against her legs, and she suppresses a cry of pain. Even standing, she can only see the top of Tim's greasy head, and only a few extra inches of his legs. Too weak to move closer, though, Jane sighs heavily as she leans against the wall while standing up. Then, she waits.

Meanwhile, the shuffling begins again, and it is much closer than before. Still with Jane unaware, it lurks right near her right foot creepily. It backs away, and the shuffling persists, and moves to the left of her. Through Jane's foggy ears, she manages to hear something else besides the erie door creaking. Just beyond the door, though, if she listens very carefully, is a heavy sliding sound, as if a heavy weight were being dragged across the surface. Jane looks around quickly to the door, only to find it slowly stop moving in the wind. She sees nothing in front of her, regardless of the lights. A gut feeling forces her to look down, and she looks at the pile of discarded newspapers near her feet, where it wasn't before.

Jane moves to the side immediately, a scream rising to her lips. She takes a step back in the direction of the door. Without looking, she reaches out towards the generator which should only be half a foot away. It isn't. Frantically, she shoots her arm out, looking for some sort of contact, while backing away slowly from the pile of newspapers. She stumbles over a dispositioned floorboard, and falls backwards on her hands.

Her focus is quickly subsided when she looks down to the right of her, and finds a single paw print on the dirty, wooden floor. Under the light of the shed, with some help from the full moon, she studies the peculiar marking. The paw print appears to belong to a wolf or coyote, but a much larger sized one. It is easily the size of her hand, or larger, and she places her frostbitten hand next to it just to compare. She looks around the floor, and notices there aren't any other footprints. This worries

Jane, and she bites down on her lip sharply to stop herself from screaming.

Jane looks at the pile of newspapers cautiously, and takes another step towards the door. She accidentally hits the corner of a table, and the side digs into her hip. Jane gasps softly in pain, while keeping her eyes trained on the pile of newspapers. It begins to shuffle around again, and Jane calls out to Tim. "T-Tim," she stutters. "I t-think there's a-an animal in here!" She shouts loudly, even though he is less than two feet away.

"Stop being such a baby," he roars quickly from behind the generator, sounding strangely loud.

His continuing insults and the situation increase Jane's frustration, and she clenches her jaw until it aches. Jane, injured, freezing, and emotional, decides to ignore him and rushes towards the shed door. "Have you gotten the generator running yet?" She asks instead, her lips shaking uncontrollably. The light overhead flickers, and she narrows her eyes at them. "Have you?"

Tim doesn't reply. The lights stream fully, and she leans closer to see Tim properly. His legs have disappeared behind the generator, but she can still see his head. It is slowly moving up and down.

"I'm not going to ask again, have you got the generator running?"

Still, no reply. Jane shuffles her feet on the ground; a mistake since her one foot is still naked, and it sends a sensation of burning, electrifying pain up her leg.

The lights flicker once more, and then quickly go out. She gasps loudly, and is relieved to see the flashlight still on. The light shines on the top of Tim's greasy black hair, but nothing else.

"I'm going back in to light a fire. We will have to wait until Ernesto comes home to fix the power." Jane says, Tim still doesn't reply. "I'm not falling for your trick, Tim. Now put the lights back on and let's go!" The pain is unbearable now, and she takes two more steps towards the front door. Nothing happens. "Fine, I'm leaving without you then." She takes two more steps towards the door, and touches the door frame lightly.

The lights turn back on, and she blinks in the sudden brightness. Jane looks behind her, and sees that Tim still has not moved an inch.

"I'll see you back in the house, I'll leave the back door open for you." She calls out, then finally takes a step into the freezing snow.

Unsure of what she was expecting, she is met with a landscape of darkness and white snow. Unable to see more than a few feet ahead of the shed, the only light coming from inside, the rest of the yard is darkness. The snow is falling even heavier now, and all she can see is puffs of snow and black. Since the power is off, she is unable to see where their manor is. Feeling hopeless, she attempts to find the large manor in the dark, going by the only light she has from within the shed. Soon, she finds herself regretting not leaving candles in the window sills.

The wind hits her face sharply, and the air is swept from her lungs. She attempts to put her sweater up around her ears, however it stupidly has no hood and does little to protect her face. As she attempts to pick her way across the painful, freezing field with only one slipper and her pajamas on, she mentally kicks every square inch of her brother, Tim.

Jane trips after a few minutes, and she lands face first in the freezing snow. She cries out as she rushes up to stand, and begins wiping off the snow. Frightened, Jane looks around. First, her eyes search for the shed, where the only light source is. Figuring from there, she can depict what direction the house is in, she sets on finding the shed once more. Just as she begins to see, what she thinks is, the shed light, it blinks once then goes out. She is encased in complete darkness. No longer able to tell what direction the house, or the shed is in now, Jane stands in the freezing cold, unsure what to do. Attempting to look for any kind of light, she turns around in circles, however, finds nothing.

6 RATHER GO BLIND

Jane stands in the snow, gobsmacked and freezing. She feels hopeless, and has every urge telling her to give up. Every inch of her body simply wants to fall and collapse into the snow. She welcomes a fast, easy death. However, the fear of lying there, for hours, waiting to be saved or waiting for death itself, scares her even more than walking around lost in the dark. She still has no idea when the sun will start rising, or when her brother will leave the shed. Nor does she know if Tim will help her when he does leave the shed. A tear drop slides down her cheek as she stares out into the darkness, her first sign of frustration and anger slipping out. "Tim?" She cries out shakily. "Where are you?" Her voice cracks on the last word, a hopeless attempt to get help.

Eerie silence follows her echoing words all around her, bouncing off of the forest surrounding their manor. Jane hears something crunch horribly nearby, and she spins towards the sound. She thinks she is looking at the source of the sound, however is unable to actually see or decipher any details. The crunching sound reaches her ears and sends shivers down her spine. Every deafening crunch sounds like a bone being taken and snapped in two like a twig, then in two more pieces right after.

Taking a shaky breath, she tries to turn towards the sound. She cries out her brother's name once more, but he is nowhere to be seen, felt or heard. She hears another crack come from her left now, and she turns towards it. Nothing; Only darkness and blizzard before her.

Jane sobs hysterically and grabs her head by her hands. Frustrated, she runs her fingers through her hair roughly. A few strands fall out, black pieces falling onto the white surface of the crusted ground. The pain on her head is strangely refreshing and acts as a wake up call to her. She begins to move away from the crunching sound, while it comes towards her. Suddenly she twirls with renewed energy and surges in the opposite direction of the bone cracking.

Jane runs at full speed, ignoring every pain in her body. She feels more of her skin blistering and peeling off, but still continues running. She knows her fingers, toes, and ears are turning black, but she still runs. There is only black and white before her, no shapes or lights, and she stretches her legs as long as they can in hopes of getting as far away from the cracking as possible.

Her legs shake and one foot falls over the other,

and Jane falls into the snow. Ice cold snow fills her nostrils and mouth, and she spits it all out. She wipes her face frantically before getting back up. She still cannot see anything, but the bone cracking sound has disappeared.

"Tim!" She calls out for her brother once more, no response.

Jane takes in a slow breath, and reaches out her arms. Using her hands as a walking stick, she slowly maneuvers herself around the field, in hopes of going in the direction of the house. The snow is now sticking to her skin, and it feels like she has ice leg warmers on her legs. Her motions are very rigid, however she has managed not to fall again.

Jane's plan is to find the fence, where she can use as a guide back to the house. She figures this is her best bet to get back inside the house blind. By the time her hand touches the wooden fence, her entire hand feels like it is about to fall off. She whimpers slightly when her hand finally does touch the fence, but a smile teases the corners of her frozen lips. Jane tries to study the fence better, in order to decipher what side of the house she is on, when she feels an engraving on one of the boards.

Jane allows her fingers to follow the familiar twirls and loops of the initials engraved in the sixteenth board on the right of the house. A smile reaches her lips, surprisingly, and a teardrop rolls down her cheek before quickly freezing. Her parents engraved their initials into the fence before she was born. However, at bedtime, they would always tell her love stories of a prince and a princess meeting. In their stories, the prince and the princess always engraved their initials into a piece of wooden; given it a tree trunk, a wooden mirror frame, or even a music box.

Jane wipes away the tears, and uses the engraving to direct her. She begins to move to the left, where the back door will be. Slowly, she uses her right hand to guide her down the fence, however is stopped midway when something furry, and warm hits her face.

7 FRESH BLOOD

Shrieking, Jane gasps as she attempts to put more space between her and the beast, however with every step she takes back, he takes one step forward. Working with the minimal light, Jane can see the creature has large, circular eyes that are mainly the colour of red, however they continue to flash ice blue. The eyes hover at least seven feet in the air, and appear to be attached to nothing. Jane hopes that is the case. Both red eyes glower down at her as she shrieks and attempts to get away. The creature reaches out with large claws, and ruins her fantasy of the creature being bodiless. The claws barely miss her, and he retracts his claw back. It disappears back into the darkness.

From where Jane stands, she can see large, circular eyes that glow. The eyes are a bright red that reminds you of fresh blood, and randomly they flash colors of ice blue. There is no iris or white of the eye, only red and blue. Hovering at least seven feet in the air Jane can not see farther than the creatures red and blue eyes. She hopes the eyes are bodiless, and are also just a figment of her imagination. Jane stands against the fence, her head frozen in position, as she hyperventilates and stares at the frightening creature.

Red eyes glower down at her, and she shrieks, unfreezing her. In seconds, she tries to rush away from the creature, in the opposite way of the back door. Hope dwindles quickly as she imagines the door getting farther and farther away.

Jane looks around frantically, and notices in the distance the shed light has come back on. She can also see footprints leaving the shed, two pairs. Just as she looks back at the creature with newfound hope, light falls on it and she can see that it does in fact have a body.

Jane watches the creature lick his jaw, and drool drips down from his long, sharp teeth. The creature looks to be a creature like a werewolf, however instead of human and wolf, it is human and lion. It is much larger than the average lion, and she can recognize human toes on the ends of its large paws, as if it hasn't finished mutating. The rest of the body looks like a lion on steroids. The tail is twice as thick, and all four legs are thick with seemingly, chemically enhanced muscle. She looks up at the ferocious creature with valid, extreme fear. She screams at the top of her lungs as the red eyes begin to advance on her. The rest of the creature's body begins to take shape, and she finds with disgust the creature has mismatched body parts instead of all lion.

It appears that someone had mismatched different types of creatures, and somehow turned them into one. She stares up at a creature with a lion's face and tail, however horns of a rhino grow from it's back, while it's torso is covered in cheetah print fur. As the creature turns slightly, Jane notices a thick armour underneath the fur.

A sound erupts from behind the creature, and it looks behind its shoulder. Seeing an opportunity, Jane turns to run in the direction of the shed. However, something halts her movement and instead she feels claws rake down the length of her back. Screaming, her body collapses on the ground, and the creature flips her onto her back. She lashes out in an attempt to fight off the beast, and her fist collides with the creatures face. The creature cries out, and she feels a frozen grin form on her face. Quickly she scurries out of the creatures reach and races in any direction. As she runs she feels her spine explode in pain, and her legs shake and struggle to move. She cries out as she continues running, unsure of what injuries wait for her.

Jane finds herself running at a tree and she quickly sideswipes it. Suddenly she finds herself running into the forest, an option she would have liked to avoid. Frustrated even more, she continues running across the forest floor and feels twigs poking up through the snow. In a rush, she bounds to the nearest full bush and hides behind it. There is a thin layer of snow covering the top of the plant, while most of the branches still have needles on them. Shakily she peers up over the top of the bush. As she searches the area, wind blows and it carries a voice to her ears. “Did you honestly think you could hide from me?” The voice says to her, it is low, almost a growl, and it sounds very familiar, however she cannot give the voice a face. While the voice sounds strangely familiar, she doesn’t let it distract her. Jane whips her head around and searches for the source.

“Tim?” She whispers and the voice laughs back at her.

“Stupid little girl. Why are you such a baby?” The voice growls and asks her. Jane freezes, her eyes widening.

“What did you say?” She asks weakly, and she skitters against the bush. Snow falls down her back, but she barely feels it.

“You never can just shut up!” The voice roars angrily at her, but the owner does not appear. Indignation and terror flare up within Jane as the words register in her mind. She thinks of her brother, and all the times he calls her a baby and screams at her to shut up. *It is so similar, the way they say it*, she thinks. *It’s so strange*.

Jane remembers the look of seeing her brother behind the generator, barely replying. She thought it was a joke. *What if the creature got to him first?* She thinks incredulously, and stifles a scream by stuffing her fist in her mouth. Her gut fills with fear while vomit threatens to rise from her stomach.

Jane takes a shaky step to the left, towards the opening of the field. In an attempt to distract the creature, she asks weakly. "What are you?" Her voice is squeaky in the night, and it barely makes its way across the wind, however the voice hears her, and suddenly the eyes appear before her.

The two red eyes reappear only a few metres away. She watches silently, fear eating her insides, as the hovering eyes near her. Her breathing comes out in short, shaky breathes, and her entire body won't stop trembling. The rest of the beast's body comes into view, and she suppresses her need to scream. It has changed, the body is now covered in scars and fresh blood. Blood drips heavily onto the snow, so warm it melts the snow it touches. While doing so, it creates a disgusting dripping sound mixed with an aroma of metal, that cause Jane to gag.

The creature picks her up suddenly, and holds her forcefully against a tree trunk, seven feet in the air. Jane can not touch the ground, and the creature's claw is digging in around her torso, creating a difficult task to breathe.

"You don't recognize me?" The creature seethes, shoving it's face in hers. She smells more blood, and vomit pours out of her mouth involuntarily. His mouth opens wide as he grows at her, and she can see pieces of chewed meat in between his sharp teeth. "We shared a womb once," the creature adds.

"What are you?!" Jane shrieks at the creature, unable to take the torture any longer. "Who are you?!" The creature growls back at her menacingly, and lifts its head to howl at the moon. Sharp dagger teeth glint at her, and she whimpers. "Please, don't hurt me." She says quickly, then a thought strikes her. Ernesto, her step-father, is a hunter. "My step-father will pay you, but if you kill me, he will hunt you. He will be home at any minute!" The words pour out of her mouth in a rush, and the creature freezes to look down at her.

"Your father?" The creature says, and he backs away, releasing his hold on her body. She falls to the ground in a heap, her legs burning even more. She cries out in pain as the creature slides away from her on his two back paws. He falls down on all fours, then disappears into the darkness. She watches his body turn and only his glowing eyes remain, he stares at her as she lays in a pile. Jane nods urgently with newfound, blazing confidence.

"That's right!" She says, in a weak but proud voice. "And if you don't leave right this minute, he's going to kill you!" Just as she thinks she has won, suddenly, in a flash, the entire creature reappears. It surges forward and grasps her small throat with his claws. She feels her skin being pierced, and then a thin trickle of blood pours down her neck. Fear stopping her from screaming, Jane falls numb as the creature pulls her down onto the ground. Her head hits the frozen pact dirt and snow hard, and she cries out in pain. Her screaming appears to entice the creature, and he cranes his neck, then howls.

8 TASTY GOOD GIRL

Jane remains silent as she watches the ground pass before her. The creature aggressively drags her body across the forest floor. She looks up at the night sky with dead eyes, watching the constellations pass before her. Her eyes wince when a sudden light appears, and she turns her neck slightly to see the light coming from the generator shed. The creature drops it's hold on her wrists, leaving thick bite marks in the skin.

While it leaves her to open the shed door, Jane's body is jolted with adrenaline and all of a sudden she's bounding towards the house again. Her body is racing, while her mind is still in the shed. She doesn't know what she is doing, however, she knows she is getting farther away from the creature.

Starting all over again, she concentrates so she does not fall this time. She breathes heavily, but doesn't lose focus. Her chest burns, and so do her feet. Everything aches, and the claw marks along her back are making her dizzy. All of her muscles are pulling with every movement she makes, and her back feels like lava is pouring down it. She wants to scream, but she doesn't, and as she sees the house appear out of the darkness she does nothing but smile.

The pavement is sharp when her feet land on it and finally she cries out in pain. Her knees shake and she finds herself falling to the pavement with numb legs. Screaming, she lands on the pavement face first and her head hits the pavement. Her head is jolted with so much pain before everything goes black momentarily. Then she's forcing herself up again. *Up,* she's telling herself. *Keep going! Don't stop,* she commands herself, unwilling to give up. All she wants to do is live. *Forget the heat,* she tells herself, *forget sleep. Just live.* The back door comes into view and she breathes out in relief.

Without warning, something takes hold of her back, and without warning her face hits the pavement. As she watches black pass over her eyesight again, a claw sweeps down her back, tearing her skin into shreds. Tensing her jaw, she bites down on her tongue and refuses to scream. She tastes blood erupt in her mouth and beginning to overfill. She spits it out hastily, and at the same time cries out in pain.

The creature does not claw her again, and she breathes out in relief. Distant footsteps can be heard, and she opens her clenched eyes to see a pair of glossy dress shoes heading her way. Looking up, she sees her step dad walking up the pathway to the house, with a sly grin on his face. At first seeing him, she felt hope rise in her chest, thinking he will save her. Instead, the look on his face says it all, and she closes her eyes with final acceptance.

"You really should listen to your father," he says harshly, and his grin disappears. Jane opens her eyes at this, and watches him carefully. He turns his gaze towards the creature, then frowns. "You've made a mess." Jane looks from her step father to the creature quickly. She begins to hyperventilate and all around her is beginning to blur. "Get off of her." Without her knowing, the creature had a giant paw on her back, pressing hard into her and forcing her lungs to no longer function properly. The creature lifts its heavy paw off of her back, leaving a sensation of pain, stinging, and air back into her lungs.

When she can breathe, she gasps. "Dad?"

His eyes move back to her, and he frowns again. "He really did make a terrible mess. That isn't good whatsoever." Then he begins to shake his head and pace. Jane looks frantically around her, unsure of what to do or what to think. Her body is pulsing and screaming at her, and she dares to never move again. However, she knows if she wants to live, she has to move, and that thought both terrifies and exhausts her.

Jane looks at the creature, who has sauntered off towards the yard. All of the lion creature's focus is on her step father, which confuses her but she won't complain.

Slowly, and quietly, she begins to move towards the back door. Her eyes frantically jump from the creature to her mysterious step father, while her heart pounds in her ears like drums. Her step father continues pacing, focused on the ground beneath him and nothing around him, while the creature watches her step father pace. When she feels the door touch her back, she winces, but a smile tugs at her lips. She takes one last look at the creature before turning around and grabbing for the knob.

Jane twists, and feels the door slide free. She pushes it open before something grabs her sweater and forces her backwards. The claws release her, and she scrambles to get through the door however the claws turn her around and she's face to face with yet another lion creature, however his fur is simply white. The white creature opens his mouth wide, revealing not one, but two rows of long incisors. Claws reach at her, and she feels her chest and throat being sliced apart. Every nerve is telling her to scream, but she can't.

A pool of blood grows around Jane, and her eyes slowly shut. Her breathing slows, and a tear drips down her cheek. As she feels her breathing slow, with every last breath, she realizes, something that chills her more than anything else that has happened.

As she watches the white creature engulf her, she realizes she never had a twin brother. Jane looks at the other creature, it's cheetah like print with eyes that flash ice blue. Ice blue that is so similar to her own, and that's what makes her know.

How could a person forget she is an only child? She asks herself, while her body slowly begins to numb. The pain ceases, and her final thought is, *how could someone forget they're an only child?* Blood spills out of her mouth as her pulse diminishes, and the creatures finally stop clawing at her.

They're mouths are covered in blood, and slowly, the cheetah print coated creature turns into a white one. His fur glints like new fallen snow. Then, it's eyes now begins to flash green instead of blue, while still blazing the bright red. The older creature begins to laugh, a coughing sound that comes out awkwardly. A pile of intestines falls out of his mouth onto the ice cold floor of the back patio. Then the smaller one follows. Slowly, the two creatures saunter away from Jane and begin their way into the woods.

Their tails swish to the side gently, and blood drips in the snow, leaving a trail. As they reach the edge of the forest, they turn back around and look at Jane for one last time. They howl, then laugh some more. Jane was the last of the Pipper family, they killed her father and then her mother. Both creatures smile terribly with their large, sharp teeth. Blood drips down each of their mouths like water from a fountain; a seemingly endless supply.

The creatures turn away and disappear into the forest. Their white fur shining brightly in the distance before also disappearing.

The creatures, called ElWolves, continue racing through the forests, their fresh prey still dripping from their lips. They laugh and the awful sound echoes throughout the forest. From miles away, another pack can hear their laugh, and they *know*. The younger ElWolf beings to run faster, and the idea of another girl, never doing wrong and then breaking a tiny little rule, that's what tastes the best. It makes him run faster, and the thought of blood runs through his mind.

ABOUT THE AUTHOR

Alexia Rowe is a student at Stratford Career Institute, working independently to increase her Creative Writing Skills. She has been engaged and actively interested in Creative Writing since childhood, and is excited about the world of fantasy and make belief. She lives in Edmonton with her family and friends, aspiring to become an inspiring author.

Printed in Great Britain
by Amazon